# LITTLE PARSLEY

To the parents
—E.G.

SIMON AND SCHUSTER BOOKS FOR YOUNG READERS
Simon & Schuster Building, Rockefeller Center,
1230 Avenue of the Americas, New York, New York 10020.

SIMON AND SCHUSTER BOOKS FOR YOUNG READERS
is a trademark of Simon & Schuster Inc.
Manufactured in the United States of America

10  9  8  7  6  5  4  3  2  1

Library of Congress Cataloging-in-Publication Data
Giannini, Enzo.   Little Parsley.
Summary: Little Parsley eludes a pack of hungry witches and
performs a series of impossible tasks with the aid of several helpers.
[1. Fairy tales. 2. Folklore—Italy.] I. Title. PZ8.G3483Li   1990
398.2'1'09455—dc19   88-19794   [E]
ISBN 0-671-67197-9

# LITTLE PARSLEY

retold and illustrated by
## ENZO GIANNINI

SIMON AND SCHUSTER BOOKS FOR YOUNG READERS
PUBLISHED BY SIMON & SCHUSTER INC., NEW YORK

ONCE UPON A TIME a husband and wife lived in a little house next to a garden that belonged to five witches. The wife was expecting a baby, and they were very happy.

One morning the woman was looking out her window into the witches' garden. She saw a patch of parsley, and at once she felt that she must have some. She waited for the witches to leave, as they did every day. Then she dropped a silken ladder from her window, climbed down into the garden, and ate parsley until she could eat no more. The next day she returned, and the next day, and the next. Indeed, she could not help herself.

One evening as the witches were strolling in their garden, the oldest witch said, "Tell me, sisters, doesn't it seem that some parsley is missing?" And the others agreed.

The next morning the witches all pretended to leave, but one remained behind, hidden in the garden.

And so it was done. No sooner had the woman climbed down the silken ladder than the witch cried out, "Ah, slyboots! I've found you out!"

The woman begged the witch to let her go, and finally the witch relented.

"We'll forgive you this time," she said, "but when your baby is born, you must call the child Little Parsley. And when it is old enough, the child will come to us and you will see it no more. Parsley you took, and parsley you must give us back, for that would only be right."

"Oh, I wish I never tasted that cursed parsley," cried the woman. She rushed home to tell her husband what had happened, and he wept, too.

Soon after, a baby girl was born, and they named her Little Parsley. As time went by the pact with the witches faded from memory. Little Parsley grew up in the house next to the garden, and when she was old enough, her parents sent her off to school.

Every day as Little Parsley passed the garden on her way
to school, the witches called out, "Little girl, tell your mother to
remember what she must give us."

"Mama," Little Parsley would say every afternoon when she returned from school, "the witches said to remind you of what you must give them." But her mother would never say a word.

One day Little Parsley's mother was busy making soup when her daughter returned from school. And this time when Little Parsley spoke, her mother answered, "Oh, tell them to take what they must."

No sooner had she spoken these terrible words than she regretted them. But already it was too late. For the words were as good as a promise and could not be undone.

After school the next day the witches were waiting as usual. "What did your mother say," they asked.

"She said for you to take what you must," answered Little Parsley.

"It's you she must give us, and now she has!" crowed the witches.

And so it was done. The witches carried the crying girl into their house and put her in a dark room where the coal was kept.

"Do you see this black, black room, Little Parsley?" said the witches. "When we return today, it must be white as milk and painted with all the birds of the air, or else we will eat you."

The witches left, and Little Parsley sank to the floor in tears. She cried a long time, until she heard a knock at the door. Could the witches be returning already? But when she opened the door it was Nino, a cousin of the witches. Little Parsley had seen him from time to time on her way to school.

"What's the matter, Little Parsley?" asked Nino. "Why are you crying so?"

"You'd cry, too," said Little Parsley, "if you had to make this black, black room as white as milk and painted with all the birds of the air, or else the witches would eat you."

"If you give me a kiss," said Nino, "I'll do it for you!" But Little Parsley answered:

> *"I'd rather be eaten by a witch*
> *Than ever by a man be kissed."*

"You said that so nicely," Nino said, sighing, "that I will help you anyway."

And with a tap of his wand the room became as white as milk, and the walls and ceilings were covered with painted birds, just as the witches had demanded.

When the witches returned, they asked, "Did you finish your task, Little Parsley?"

"Yes, ma'ams," she answered.

The witches stared at each other in amazement. "Ah, Little Parsley, was our cousin Nino here?"

But Little Parsley answered:

*"Nino is no one that I know,*
*My dear Mama will tell you so!"*

"Is that so, little girl," said the witches suspiciously. "Let's see how you fare with this next task. Tomorrow you must go to the palace of the Witch Morgana. Tell her to give you the box of the Royal Jester and bring it back here."

"Yes, ma'ams," said Little Parsley.

And so the next morning she set out on her way. She walked and walked, and there in the middle of her path she found Nino.

"And where are you going, Little Parsley?" he asked.

"I'm going to the palace of the Witch Morgana to get the box of the Royal Jester."

"Then you had better take these gifts for those you will meet along the way," said Nino. "Here are two pots of lard, for on your road you will find two doors that squeak and grind. And here are two loaves of bread, for you will meet two dogs that bite each other. Here is some twine and an awl, for you will meet a cobbler who sews shoes with lengths of his beard and hair. And take these brushes, for you will meet a baker who sweeps her oven with her hands."

And so it was done. Little Parsley did as she was told
and the doors, the dogs, the cobbler, and the baker
all let her pass by.

Just down the road from the Witch Morgana's palace, Little Parsley found Nino waiting for her.

"And now," he said, "when you knock at the door of the palace, the Witch Morgana will say, 'Wait, little girl. Wait just a minute.' But you must climb the big stairs as fast as you can, take the box at the top of the second staircase, and run! For if she catches you, she'll eat you."

And so it was done.

Hearing the girl run away, the Witch Morgana leaned out her window and yelled, "Oh baker who sweeps her oven with her hands, stop that girl! Stop her!"

The witch called to the dogs that bite each other, "Stop that girl, stop her!"

"We would be fools!" said the dogs. "She brought us bread, a loaf for each. Run, little one, run!"

"Oh doors that squeak and grind, stop that girl!"

"We won't," said the doors. "She has greased us from top to bottom. Run, little one, run!"

"Do you think I'm a fool?"
cried the baker. "She gave me
brushes for my oven.
Run, little one, run!"

"Oh cobbler who sews with beard
and hair," called the witch, "stop that girl!
Stop her!"
     "Not I. She brought me all that
I need! Run, little one, run!"

When she was safe at last, Little Parsley stopped to rest. "I wonder what is in this box?" she asked herself. Little Parsley opened the box and…

…out popped hundreds of tiny men, playing musical instruments and marching in all directions. As fast as she would put one back in the box, ten more would hop out.

"Oh, how will I put them all back?" she cried, and then she saw Nino.

"Peeping Parsley," he exclaimed, "what have you done?"

"I just wanted a peek…." sniffed Little Parsley.

"Ah," said Nino, "a peek…and now what shall you do? If you give me a kiss, I'll put everything in order."

But Little Parsley answered:

> "I'd rather be eaten by a witch
> Than ever by a man be kissed."

"Oh, well," Nino said, sighing, "you said that so nicely that I'll do it anyway." And with a tap of his wand, all the tiny musicians were returned to the box.

Little Parsley went back to the house of the witches and knocked at the door.

The witches had seen her coming. "Oh, badness," they said. "It's Little Parsley! So the Witch Morgana didn't eat her!"

"Ah," said the oldest witch, "it must be that Little Parsley is for us to eat." And the others agreed.

That evening Nino stopped by the house of the witches. "You know, Nino," they said, "the Witch Morgana didn't eat Little Parsley. She left her for us to eat!"

"Is that so?" said Nino.

"Tomorrow when she has finished her chores, we will tell her to put a fire under a big pot, the one for doing laundry. And when it's boiling, we'll take her and throw her in."

"Yes, yes," said Nino. "You must do exactly that."

The next morning after the witches had all left as they did every day, Nino went to find Little Parsley. "Little Parsley," he said, "today the witches will tell you to make a fire under a big laundry pot, for they plan to throw you in and cook you! But you must say that you need to fetch firewood from the cellar. Go there and you'll find me."

And so it was done.

"Be brave," whispered Nino to Little Parsley when they found each other in the dark of the cellar. He took her hand and led her to a far and lost corner where there were many candles glowing.

"These are the souls of the witches," said Nino, "and the biggest one is the soul of the Witch Morgana. Blow, Little Parsley, blow with all your strength, and they will be gone forever."

Together they blew and blew and blew out all the candles, even the great big one...and the witches were no more.

"And now you should marry me, for that would only be right," said Nino.

"I will," said Little Parsley. And this time he did not have to ask for a kiss, for Little Parsley gave him one freely.

All of the wealth of the witches was left to them. The house and garden of the witches they gave to Little Parsley's mother and father, for her mother had long repented her careless words. Nino and Little Parsley married, and off they went to the palace of the Witch Morgana. The cobbler they made a duke, the baker a countess. They kept the dogs with them at the palace, and the doors were always well greased.